THE ONLY LIVIN[G]

BENEATH THE UNSEEN CITY

by David Gallaher and Steve Ellis

PAPERCUTZ™
New York

To Vanessa, Rory, and Lolo, the
superest of superheroes. I love and
adore you all.
—David

To my wife Yamila, beautiful and
strong, who believes in me even
when I can't. I love you!
—Steve

THE ONLY LIVING GIRL #2 "Beneath the Unseen City"

Chapters 3 & 4
Writer/Co-Creator: David Gallaher
Artist/Co-Creator: Steve Ellis
Colors: Steve Ellis
Color Flatting: Sarah Elkins, Sigi Ironmonger, Holley McKend
Color Corrections: Sarah Elkins
Lettering: Nate Pride
Studio Assistant: Jen Lightfoot
Special Thanks to Dara Hyde, Jeff Whitman, Vanessa Shealy, the
tremendous team at Papercutz and all of our outstanding readers.

Serialized at: www.onlylivinggirl.com

All other editorial material © 2020 Papercutz.
www.papercutz.com

Publication rights for this edition arranged
through Papercutz and Hill Nadell Agency.

Papercutz books may be purchased for business or promotional
use. For information on bulk purchases please contact Macmillan
Corporate and Premium Sales Department at
(800) 221-7945 x5442.

Production – JayJay Jackson
Cover Logo – Adam Grano and Dawn Guzzo
Editorial Intern – Izzy Boyce-Blanchard
Managing Editor – Jeff Whitman
Jim Salicrup
Editor-in-Chief

PB ISBN: 978-1-6299-1055-0
HC ISBN: 978-1-6299-1056-7

Printed in China
February 2020

Distributed by Macmillan
First Printing

CHAPTER THREE

Previously in...

THE ONLY LIVING GIRL

Zee Parfitt slept through the apocalypse.

Her father, Doctor Thomas Parfitt, made a deal with a group of devilish scientists called the Consortium to save his daughter's life after a car tragically hit her. This deal saved Zee by putting her to sleep in suspended animation, but it also transformed the world into the patchwork planet of Chimerika, and warped her father into the deranged Doctor Once, who ravaged the planet's inhabitants with his evil experiments. The only living boy, Erik Farrell, and his allies vanquished Doctor Once, imprisoned Baalikar, and finally awakened Zee.

Now, six months later, Erik, Zee, her trusty companion Bear, and their Mermidonian warrior-ally Morgan are living in Stronghold and working with the newly-formed World Alliance. When a techno-organic being named Lumino arrives at Stronghold, he accidentally poisons the Alliance's Science Team with Afterall radiation. He explains that Afterall was recently discovered by the Consortium, and they are using it to destroy the world. Their planet's only hope is for Zee, Erik, Bear, and Morgan to venture across a treacherous sea to an invisible city in search of the only thing that can save them - the Primordial Intelligence.

CHAPTER FOUR

WATCH OUT FOR PAPERCUTZ™

Welcome to the second, spine-tingling THE ONLY LIVING GIRL graphic novel, "Beneath the Unseen City," by writer/co-creator David Gallaher and artist/co-creator Steve Ellis, brought to you by Papercutz, the Earth-bound tribe of humans dedicated to publishing great graphic novels for all ages. I'm Jim Salicrup, the Editor-in-Chief and Patchwork-Person, here to help newcomers to this strange wonderful world of THE ONLY LIVING GIRL...

It all began with the critically-acclaimed THE ONLY LIVING BOY webcomic by David Gallaher and Steve Ellis. It was in this webcomic that everything regarding Erik Farrell and Zee Parfitt started. If you've been following the Papercutz graphic novels, then you're already up-to-speed, but for those of you just joining us, it's easy to catch up. You can go to www.the-only-living-boy.com and that'll take you through the story of Erik Farrell, THE ONLY LIVING BOY.

Or you could pick up the five volume THE ONLY LIVING BOY series available at booksellers everywhere and at your local public or school library. These books collect the webcomic in five volumes.

Or you could get THE ONLY LIVING BOY OMNIBUS, which not only collects the five graphic novels, but includes THE ONLY LIVING BOY FREE COMIC BOOK DAY comic and features another all-new THE ONLY LIVING BOY story. This book is also available at booksellers everywhere and at your local public or school library.

Following THE ONLY LIVING BOY series is THE ONLY LIVING GIRL, focused on Zee Parfitt. Once you've caught up on THE ONLY LIVING BOY, then all you need is the first THE ONLY LIVING GIRL graphic novel, and you're totally up to speed. Even if you missed that, don't worry, as there's a handy re-cap on page 4 that gives you everything you'll need to know to enjoy "Beneath the Unseen City."

Most Papercutz graphic novels are self-contained, meaning they tell a complete story or several stories all in one graphic novel. But THE ONLY LIVING GIRL is a little different. Like the blockbuster Marvel movies, where each movie (except for that Avengers 2-parter) tells a complete story, each of THE ONLY LIVING GIRL graphic novels tells a complete story, but it's also a piece of a much bigger story. The good news is, that unlike Marvel, you don't need to catch up on eighty years of comics or ten years of movies – this is just the six graphic novels chronicling the adventures of Erik and Zee! Shouldn't take that long to catch up, right?

In fact, knowing how bright our fans are, we imagine that six graphic novels isn't quite enough to completely satisfy your appetite for extraordinary adventure stories. Well, ever-thinking Papercutz was able to anticipate that this might be a concern, and we're happy to announce two new Papercutz series that will rocket you to the future and plummet you back to the past for more action, adventure, and fun! First, there's...

SCHOOL FOR EXTRATERRESTRIAL GIRLS – An all-new graphic novel series co-created by Jeremy Whitley, writer (he's the creator of *Princeless*, and the writer of Marvel's *Future Foundation*) and Jamie Noguchi, artist, about a 15-year-old girl, Tara Smith, who suddenly discovers that everything she thought she knew about herself was a lie. That she's not even a human being – that she's actually an alien. And that's when she finds herself enrolled in the SCHOOL FOR EXTRATERRESTRIAL GIRLS.

© 2020 Jeremy Whitley and Jamie Noguchi.

Then there's...

ASTERIX – If this series sounds familiar, it may be because ASTERIX is one of the most popular and best-selling comics series in the world. Created by René Goscinny, writer, and Albert Uderzo, artist, sixty years ago, Papercutz is proud to become the new North American publisher of this classic comics series. Asterix, for those of you who may be unfamiliar with him, is a scrappy warrior in a small village in Gaul, in the year 50 BC. Somehow Asterix and his village have managed to fend off the Roman Empire from conquering them. How could this tiny warrior and this tiny village possibly survive against such overwhelming odds? Turns out they have a secret weapon – a power potion that gives every member of their village super-strength. That doesn't stop the Romans from trying to defeat Asterix and his friends... and the stories of their endless battles are both exciting and lots of fun. Asterix also has plenty of other adventures back then as he travels all over the world and you can experience them all in ASTERIX, as well.

That ought to keep you busy until your next appointment with THE ONLY LIVING GIRL #3 "In the Presence of Doctor Twice." If not, you can always go to www.papercutz.com to find even more incredible graphic novels!

Thanks, *Jim*

Asterix® © 2020 Les Éditions Albert
René/Goscinny-Uderzo

STAY IN TOUCH!

EMAIL: salicrup@papercutz.com
WEB: papercutz.com
INSTAGRAM: @papercutzgn
TWITTER: @papercutzgn
FACEBOOK: PAPERCUTZGRAPHICNOVELS
FAN MAIL: Papercutz, 160 Broadway, Suite 700,
             East Wing, New York, NY 10038